MILLIONS OF YEARS AGO

prehistoric *TRUCKS* roamed the earth.

They were **HUGE**.

They were **HUNGRY**.

But they weren't helpful like they are today.

They rumbled, roared, and chomped.

And they did *NOT* get along well with others.

They were called . . .

Little, Brown Books for Young Readers • Hachette Book Group
237 Park Avenue, New York, NY 10017
Visit our Web site at www.lb-kids.com

Little, Brown Books for Young Readers is a division of
Hachette Book Group, Inc.
The Little, Brown name and logo are trademarks of
Hachette Book Group, Inc.

First Edition: June 2009

Library of Congress Cataloging-in-Publication Data
Gall, Chris.
Dinotrux / written and illustrated by Chris Gall.—1st ed.
p. cm.
Summary: Millions of years ago, the prehistoric ancestors of today's
trucks, such as Garbageadon, Dozeratops, and Craneosaurus, roamed the
Earth until they rusted out and became extinct.
ISBN 978-0-316-02777-9
[1. Imaginary creatures-Fiction. 2. Trucks-Fiction.] 1. Title.
PZ7.G1352Tr 2009
[E]—dc22
2008027531

10 9 8 7 6 5 4 3 2 1

SC • Printed in China

The text was set in Cafeteria Black, and the display type
is hand-lettered. The artwork for this book was created
using bearskins and stone knives.

LITTLE, BROWN AND COM
Books for Young Reade
New York   Boston

The earth was **FIERY** and **DANGEROUS**.
Volcanoes shot lava everywhere.
Cave people ran for their lives—
and tar pits could swallow them whole.

LOOK! High in the branches . . .

CRANEOSAURUS!

He was always sticking his nose
where it didn't belong.

CRACK, MUNCH.

Look out, birds, it's time for lunch!

There goes **ROLLODON!**
He **NEVER** watches where he's going.

GARBAGEADON

ate everything in sight.

GOBBLE!
GOBBLE!

Be careful,
caveman!

RUMBLE! RUMBLE! RUMBLE!

A **SEMISAUR** stampede!

All night long, always in a hurry . . .

Everybody run!

CHOMPING, ROLLING, DIGGING,

HONKING . . .

the Dinotrux ruled for a million years or more.
But one day, there was a flash of light and a terrible storm.

Dinotrux everywhere **WHEEZED** and **SNEEZED.**
Most began to rust.
They slowly sank into the goo and mud.

But the smart ones went south in search of better weather.

And over the **HUNDREDS**

and **THOUSANDS**

and **MILLIONS** of years,

And they never, **EVER** quit!

T. TRUX